Hammy

🐾 Elizabeth Dale 🐾

Illustrated by Harmen van Straaten

ORCHARD BOOKS

For Evelyn Mansfield, with love
ED
For Maggie Mundy
HvS

ORCHARD BOOKS
96 Leonard Street, London EC2A 4RH
Orchard Books Australia
14 Mars Road, Lane Cove, NSW 2066
First published in Great Britain in 1999
First Paperback Edition 2000
Text © Elizabeth Dale 1999
Illustrations © Harmen van Straaten 1999
The rights of Elizabeth Dale to be identified as the author
and Harmen van Straaten as the illustrator of this work
have been asserted by them in accordance with the
Copyright, Designs and Patents Act, 1988.
A CIP catalogue record for this book is available
from the British Library.
1 3 5 7 9 10 8 6 4 2 (hardback)
1 3 5 7 9 10 8 6 4 2 (paperback)
1 86039 796 4 (hardback)
1 86039 797 2 (paperback)
Printed in Great Britain

CONTENTS

Paul's Secret

As Paul walked to school that cold, grey Friday morning, he couldn't help but smile. For weeks now he'd been cherishing a secret, all to himself, and soon, very soon, he would share it with everyone.

His class were gathered in a huddle in the playground. Paul ran over to meet them. There was only one possible topic of conversation.

"Pet Week next week!" cried Sam, as if everyone didn't know. "I can't wait to bring Geronimo in. Everyone will love him! He's the best dog in the world, and the biggest. He's sleek and strong and clever. He's so intelligent, I'm sure he understands what I'm saying."

"Intelligent?" laughed Robbie, bouncing his football up and down. "He's the daftest dog around!"

"He only acts silly to make me laugh," said Sam. "He's so cute, he's adorable…"

Paul took a deep breath. This was it. The time to tell everyone. "I'm bringing in my pet." he said, quietly.

"And he has the most beautiful deep brown eyes…" continued Sam.

"What was that you said, Titch?" asked Tessa, turning to look at Paul.

Paul scowled at her. He hated being called Titch, and everyone knew it. But somehow everyone in his class carried on calling him it, just because he was so small. He couldn't help it.

"Did you say *your* pet?" asked Tessa.

Paul smiled as he thought of Hammy. "Yes, I'm bringing my pet into Pet Week," he repeated.

"*Your* pet?" asked Sam. He was rather annoyed about being interrupted when he was telling everyone about Geronimo, but at the same time he was intrigued. "You've never got a pet, have you?" he asked.

"Yes!" said Paul proudly.

"You didn't tell us!" said Robbie. "I didn't think you were allowed pets in your house. What is it?"

Paul grinned at them. This was the moment he'd been waiting for, the chance to show off about Hammy, the way Sam always did about Geronimo.

"No, don't tell us, let's guess!" said Sam. "What kind of pet do you think Titch would have? He'd have to have something small, otherwise it would be bigger than him! Let me think…it's a goldfish, isn't it? Or a newt?"

"Don't pick on him!" said Robbie. "What have you got, Paul? Is it a kitten? You always wanted a cat. Why have you never told us about her before?"

Paul opened his mouth and then closed it again. There was one good reason why he'd never told anyone about Hammy. He just knew everyone would joke about how small he was, and how he suited his owner perfectly. Why was size so important, anyway? It was what was inside that counted and Hammy was so inquisitive, intelligent and funny.

"What's her name?"asked Robbie.

"Hamish," said Paul. "Hammy for short. It's a he. He's very clever and he has the most amazing soft fur."

"Ah, he's a hairy newt!" cried Sam, and Tessa giggled.

"He's not!" said Paul. "He's a –"

"Well?" said Sam. "What is he?"

"You'll have to wait and see," said Paul. "I'll bring him in next week."

"Go on!" said Sam. "You can't leave it like that."

"Yes I can!" grinned Paul. And he knocked Robbie's football out of his hand and ran after it. "Come on!" he cried over his shoulder. "Who's for a game before the bell goes?"

Hammy goes to School

Finally Pet Week arrived. Paul could hardly sleep on the Sunday night, he was so excited, and yet…

"So today's the big day," said his mum as Paul nibbled a bit of toast the next morning. "The day you show Hammy to the world."

"Um…I'm not sure," said Paul. He looked over to where his pet lay asleep in the corner of the kitchen. "All the noise at school might frighten him."

"Come on!" said his mum. "All you've talked about since we got him is how you could take him into school in Pet Week."

"I know…" said Paul.

"They'll all love him!" said his mum.

11

"Look at his gorgeous honey-coloured fur."

Paul smiled. She was right. Everyone would think that Hammy was adorable.

"All right!" he said. "I'll show Sam that there are other animals in this world besides his precious Geronimo!"

"I'll take you both in the car," said his mum. "It'll be easier that way."

Unfortunately Paul's mum's car wouldn't start at first and they got to school late. Everyone was in the classroom, stroking Tessa's rabbit, Anne-Marie's kitten and Robbie's snake. Sam was keeping a tight hold on Geronimo at the other end of the classroom, just in case he decided that he hadn't had enough breakfast! No one saw

Paul walk in with Hammy, no one except Miss Biggs.

"Oh, Paul!" she cried. "What a super pet!"

Everyone turned and looked at Hammy.

"Ah!" cried Julia. "Isn't he gorgeous?"

"How cute!" sighed Robbie.

But above them all yelled Sam. "I knew it!" he yelled. "Trust Titch to have a tiny little rat!"

Paul went red. "It isn't a rat, it's a hamster!" he said, glaring at Sam.

Geronimo barked loudly and in an instant, Hammy scurried back inside his nest.

"It's even a cowardly hamster!" laughed Sam. "Be quiet, Geronimo, it's not even big enough to have for your mid-morning snack!"

Paul wanted to cry. This was just the kind of reaction he'd dreaded. No one liked Hammy.

But then Julia said, "Oh, isn't he sweet, Titch? Can I hold him, please?"

"Look at his little nose peeking out," said Tessa. "And his whiskers twitching."

"Does he bite?" asked Robbie. He put his finger to the cage and Hammy sniffed at it.

"Savaged by a hamster!" laughed Sam. "Oh, help! Save me! What a terrible fate!"

Geronimo started barking again as everyone joined in with Sam's laughter. He got so excited, he pulled his lead out of Sam's hand and with his big tail started knocking papers and books flying. A vase of flowers went crashing to the floor, sending tulips and water everywhere, and Julia's goldfish nearly followed them.

"Sam Brown! If you can't keep your dog under better control, we'll have to send for your mum to take him home," said Miss Biggs severely.

Sam stopped laughing and glared at Paul. It was all his silly fault.

Geronimo!

All the pets in bowls, tanks and cages were
put on top of the shelves under the
window. It was great to see them there.
Every time Paul had a problem with his
sums, he looked across at
Hammy sleeping
quietly in his
bundle of
bedding, his
little nose
just peeping out,
and immediately he felt better.
Everyone had loved him, apart from Sam.
But then, as far as Sam was concerned,
there was no animal on this earth as good
as Geronimo.

But Miss Biggs didn't agree. Geronimo was far too excited by all the children to settle down quietly in a corner. No sooner had he been told off for one thing and been taken back to his bean bag and told firmly to stay there, than he'd suddenly decide there was another interesting smell to go and investigate. Finally Miss Biggs took him to the back and tied him to the big rubber plant in the corner.

Paul looked across at Hammy who was behaving perfectly, curled up in his cage, quiet and happy. What a wonderful pet he was!

"Let's do some tables!" said Miss Biggs. "Who knows three times eight? Yes, Tessa?"

"I don't know, miss," she said. "But I think Geronimo's about to eat Julia's goldfish!"

"What!" cried Miss Biggs. "Stop him, Robbie! Quick!"

Robbie tried. He reached for Geronimo with one hand, while Julia grabbed her goldfish bowl with two. Just in time! But then Geronimo started trying to dig up the rubber plant instead, so Miss Biggs tied him to her desk so she could keep an eye on him. For a while he was fine, but when everyone came back in after assembly and discovered that he'd eaten half the names in Miss Biggs's register, their teacher had had enough.

"Sam Brown, this is the last straw!" she cried as she strode towards Geronimo. But it wasn't. A sensible dog would have known by just one look at Miss Biggs's face that she wasn't playing. But Geronimo was not a sensible dog. He bounced around, his tail wagging, hitting Zak in the face and knocking his glasses off. Everyone fell about with laughter. Miss Biggs stepped forward, grabbing for his lead. She'd almost got it, when, whoosh! She slid right over, flat on her back. Class 3W tried to stop laughing, they were sure they'd be in terrible trouble, but they just couldn't help themselves.

"Who's spilt something slippery on this floor?" Miss Biggs demanded angrily, sitting up. And then her nose wrinkled up, and she twisted and looked at what she was sitting in.

"Oh, pooh!" cried Julia, who was the nearest to her.

"Disgusting!" said Robbie, holding his nose.

"Geronimo!" said Miss Biggs faintly.

Sam didn't wait to be told. He grabbed hold of Geronimo's lead and took him outside. Geronimo hadn't quite been the big hit he'd hoped for.

Hammy is a Hit

4

After first break, when Sam's mum fetched Geronimo, and Miss Biggs had had time to go home, get changed and drink two soothing cups of tea, the whole room reeked of disinfectant as the class settled down to talk about pet week once more.

"Now then, who wants to be the first to tell us about their pet?" asked Miss Biggs.

Robbie told everyone about how his snake hibernated in winter and then Tessa described how she took her rabbit for a walk on a lead but the only problem was that it could run faster than her. Anne-Marie demonstrated how her kitten could switch on the light all on his own.

"You see, every pet is clever is some way," said Miss Biggs as everyone clapped.

"Titch's hamster isn't," said Sam. "All it's done is sleep. But then, they do say pets take after their owners."

"That's why Geronimo did a whatsit on our floor, is it?" said Robbie, and everyone laughed.

"Actually, Hammy is very clever," said Paul, standing up. "It's just that he sleeps in the day time. At night he's very active."

"What's the use of that?" asked Sam, determined to get his own back. "You're asleep at night so you don't see it."

"My kitten, Clarissa, can climb up the curtains," said Anne-Marie. "And when the phone rings she knocks the receiver off and miaows into it."

"Purr-fect!" giggled Julia.

"Hammy can empty his water bottle just by nudging it, and then he knocks it out and—"

"Look!" cried Anne-Marie. Everyone was distracted by her cat climbing up the classroom curtains.

"Isn't she clever!" cried Robbie.

"Can she get down by herself?" asked Miss Biggs anxiously.

Paul stood there. No one wanted to hear about how clever his hamster was. He thought it was absolutely brilliant the way Hammy knocked all the water out of his bottle. And then, when it was light enough, he pushed the bottle out of the cage and climbed out of the hole left by the water bottle. He then went all over the house. Talk about being a clever climber!

Talk about adventurous!

"My pet escapes at night!" he said when Clarissa was safely back in Anne-Marie's arms. "He scurries around the house collecting things and taking them back to his nest."

"Really?" asked Miss Biggs. "What kind of things?"

"My sister, Jenny, has little plastic play people. Hammy collects them from their play house, takes them back to his cage and snuggles up with them in his nest."

"Ah! How cute!" cried Anne-Marie.

"How clever!" said Miss Biggs, and Paul smiled.

"Can you train him to do anything?" asked Tessa.

"Oh, yes," said Paul. "He didn't like being handled at first – he bit me the first time I held him – but Mum said that was because he was scared and wasn't used to me. So I trained him to get used to me: I opened his cage each night, just as he was waking up, and took him in my hands and stroked him gently. Now he's there every night at the door waiting for me. And, once he's out, he climbs all over me. It's like I'm an obstacle course. He runs up my sleeve and it tickles!"

Everyone laughed, except Sam, but Paul didn't notice. Everyone was interested now. There was no doubt about it, Hammy was a hit. Paul told the class how Hammy, like all hamsters, liked living on his own away from other hamsters. He had everything he needed in his cage, a nest, his food, water, a wheel to run around and a bit of wood to chew on. Everyone seemed impressed, apart from Sam, who was upset that Geronimo had been taken home and his moment of glory had gone.

"What a wimp!" he said as they walked out for dinner. "Trust Titch to have a pet who plays with silly dolls. Geronimo may be a bit naughty, but at least he's fun. You never know what he's going to do next! Look, your little rat is so exciting it hasn't woken up all morning!"

Paul glared at Sam. Hammy was the best pet in the world and Paul was proud of

him. Hammy might be small, but so was
Paul, and small was OK. At least that's
what Paul kept telling himself.

Oh, Hammy!

The next morning, Paul's whole family overslept, even Jenny, who usually woke the whole house up.

"Why didn't you wake me?" cried Paul's dad, running downstairs.

Paul rubbed his eyes and gazed sleepily at his mum. It was going to be one of those mornings.

Paul's mum gave his dad a cup of coffee. "Calm down." she said. "We're not that far behind time."

"OK," Paul's dad said, munching a piece of toast, "I'll just ring the office to tell them I'll be late." He picked up the receiver and frowned.

"The phone isn't working!" he cried, staring at it.

"Well it was all right last night," said Paul's mum.

"Maybe the lines are down?" said his dad, fiddling with the phone, and then he saw it. "Look!" he said, pointing. The telephone wire was cut through.

"Who did this?" he demanded. "Paul! You've been messing around with your scissors again."

"It wasn't me!" said Paul. He looked at his little sister.

"I didn't do it." Jenny said.

"Well, I didn't do it," continued Paul's dad, still looking at Paul. "And neither did your mum, and Jenny is too small to have the strength. Who else could it have been?"

"*I* didn't do it!" said Paul. "Honest!"

Paul's mum took his hand. "Darling," she said, "no one else has been in the flat. Look, the ends of the wires are sharp, they have been deliberately cut. Unless…" She frowned suddenly and looked around her. "Do you think someone could have broken in? There *have* been a lot of burglaries around here lately."

"I'll check," said Paul's dad. He had a quick look around the house. "There's nothing missing," he said, returning "no windows forced...I just don't understand it. But this settles it. I'm getting a burglar alarm on my way to work. Right now. Bye!" He grabbed his briefcase and rushed out of the door.

Paul's mum watched him go and then turned back to her son. She frowned. "Paul," she said quietly, sitting down with him, "there weren't any burglars last night. No one came into this house. You can own up now and I won't be cross. Maybe you didn't mean to cut right through the phone wire, perhaps you were just messing around and your scissors were sharper than you thought...?"

"I wasn't!" cried Paul. "I didn't play with my scissors yesterday! I didn't cut through the phone wires. Honest!"

Paul's mum looked at him and shook her head. "Now I think about it…I made a phone call after you'd gone to bed," she said slowly. "The wire must have been cut after then, after I'd gone to bed. But no one was up in the night except…Oh dear!"

She turned and looked at Hammy's cage, where he was sleeping peacefully curled round one of Jenny's toys. Paul went pale. Oh no! It couldn't be…could it? He looked at his mum and then back to the cage in horror. The water bottle was on the floor, leaving a gaping hole in the top of the cage. Hammy must have escaped during the night. It had to be him. Who else could it be?

Hammy, be Good

🐾
6

"Paul Stevens!" cried his dad that night
when his mum told him about Hammy.
"That hamster is going to have to go!"

"No!" cried Paul. "Oh Dad, please!"

"We've got the phone reconnected today, so that's back to normal," said his mum. "I'm sure Paul can fix the water bottle so that Hammy can't push it out and escape from his cage, can't you, Paul?"

Paul smiled at her gratefully. "I will!" he said. "I will! I'll do it right now."

"Hmmm!" said his dad. "Well, OK then, but make sure you fix it properly. We were lucky last night. What if it hadn't been the phone wire Hammy had nibbled through? What if he'd bitten through a live cable...?"

Paul stared at his dad, horrified. "Hammy could have electrocuted himself, couldn't he?" he asked. "He could have been killed!"

"Worse than that," said his dad. "There might have been a fire. He could have set fire to the flat! We could all have gone up in flames!"

Paul frowned. He couldn't bear to think

about it. Poor Hammy! He was just too adventurous for his own good.

While his dad went to try to fix the new burglar alarm, Paul knelt down by Hammy's cage and carefully stuck down the water bottle with sticky tape. He used nearly half a roll trying to make the bottle secure.

"That looks good," said his mum when he'd finished. "Don't worry, Paul, everything will be all right. Your dad would never make you get rid of Hammy. He knows how much you love him. Why don't you offer to go and help him with the burglar alarm? From the way he's thumping around in the lounge, it sounds as if he's having terrible trouble with it."

"OK!" grinned Paul.

His mum was right. Paul's dad was completely surrounded by a jumble of wires.

"I've fixed Hammy's water bottle," said Paul. "He won't be able to get out any more. Can I help you now?"

His dad smiled up at Paul. "No thanks," he said. "I think I'll leave this for tonight and have another go tomorrow when I've got more time. Do you want to hear the noise it makes when it goes off?"

Paul nodded his head.

His dad put two wires together. RINGGG! The noise made Paul jump half a mile.

"Think it's loud enough?" his dad asked, turning it off.

"It's probably woken the dead in the churchyard!" said Paul.

"Let's hope Hammy doesn't nibble it to pieces in the night!" his dad said.

"He won't!" promised Paul. To be sure, before he went to bed, he took Hammy out and cuddled him and told him to stay in his cage that night. He stroked him and held him close.

"I don't know what I'd do if I had to get rid of you," he said. "Please, Hammy, please be good. For my sake!"

Burgled!

RING!! Paul woke up with a jump. The noise was so loud, it was deafening.
RING! RING!
RIIIING!!

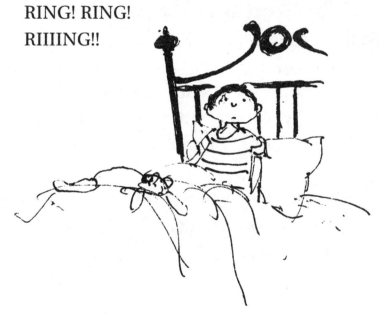

"What the blazes!" cried his dad.
Paul jumped out of bed.

Jenny was crying, but he ran straight past her room and downstairs, following his dad. When they opened the lounge door, they both stood still and stared in horror. It was as though a bomb had hit it. There were chairs knocked over, drawers pulled out, papers all over the floor, and there in the middle, next to the burglar alarm, was Hammy, chewing away.

Paul couldn't believe it. He felt as though a knife was twisting in his heart. No! Hammy had really done it this time! He turned to his dad, tears pricking at his eyes.

"Hammy didn't mean to do all this!" he said. "He must have had a brainstorm! Perhaps I've been giving him too many nuts to eat. He…" What could he say?

His dad turned to him, shaking his head slowly.

"Hammy didn't do this, son," he said.

"He's only tiny. We've been burgled. Look the TV's gone. And the video."

Paul sat down. No! Not the video! His mum walked in, carrying Jenny.

"Oh no!" she cried. "What a mess!"

Paul's dad opened the door to the front hall. "Hold on!" he cried. "Look at this!" Paul ran after him and peered over his shoulder. There, stacked by the front door, were two radios, the microwave, a camera, the TV and the video.

"They put them there, ready to take,"

said Paul's dad. "But when the alarm went off they fled empty-handed. It looks as though they haven't taken a thing."

"What luck!" said his mum. "The alarm went off just in time. But what on earth set it off?"

Everyone looked at the alarm, left where Paul's dad had finished with it the night before. Hammy was still sniffing around it. They looked at Hammy. And then they looked at each other.

"Hammy!" they cried, and Paul ran and

picked him up. "You clever thing!" he said.

"He's nibbled through the insulation on the wires," said his dad. "Hammy must have knocked them together and made the alarm go off. What a clever hamster! It's a good job you aren't very clever at sticking his bottle back in, Paul!"

Paul grinned.

"What a star!" cried his mum.

"Don't touch anything else," said his

dad. "I'll go and ring the police."

"I take it I can make a cup of tea?" asked Paul's mum, walking into the kitchen.

"I don't see why not—" Paul's dad was interrupted by a scream from the kitchen.

"What is it?" he cried.

"My rings!" said Paul's mum. "My engagement ring and my eternity ring. I took them off when I was doing the washing-up last night and left them by the sink. And now they've gone!"

Paul ran to see if they were by the front door with all the other things. But they weren't.

"The thieves must have taken them,"
said his dad, putting his arm around Paul's
mum. "All they had to do was slip them in
their pockets. I'm sorry, love, they've gone!
I don't suppose we'll ever see them again."

Everyone sat down. Paul's mum wiped a
tear from her eye. "I know they're
insured," she said. "I'll get my money
back. But nothing can ever replace those
rings. They mean so much to me."

The police, when they came, agreed that
they would be unlikely to
track down the rings.

"These are
professional
thieves," they
said. "There's a
big market
in stolen jewels:
they'll take the
stones out and
sell them
separately.
Even if we should find the
robbers, they've probably got rid of the
jewels by now."

"Oh dear," said Paul's mum.

"At least they didn't take anything else," said the policeman. "Thanks to that clever hamster of yours."

"All my years in the force, I've never heard anything like it," said his colleague. "Fancy him setting the alarm off like that, scaring them off. Just to lose your rings, when the burglars could have taken everything. You were very lucky."

But Paul's mum didn't feel very lucky. She tried to smile, but Paul knew that she'd rather the burglars had taken everything else but her rings.

Once the policemen had gone, Paul made his mum a cup of tea. And then he went and took Hammy out of his cage and stroked him again. Cuddling Hammy always helped when he felt bad.

Half an hour later, the
fingerprint men
came and put their
powder all over
everything,
trying to
find some
good prints,
something to help the police track down
the robbers. They took copies of all the
family's fingerprints
too, and it soon
became clear that
the burglars
hadn't left any
of their own.
Finally the men
finished and
they gave
permission for the
mess to be tidied up.

Paul's dad suggested that Paul and
Jenny went back to bed, but Paul knew he
wouldn't sleep. Instead, he helped put
everything right.
Finally, he went
to say good night
to Hammy, who
was scurrying
around in
his cage.

"You clever
boy!" he said
as Hammy
came up to the
door to sniff at
Paul's finger.

Paul opened the door and let Hammy run on to his open hand. He looked at the broken tape that had once held the water bottle in place. Hammy must have had a real battle to get through that and escape from his cage!

"Do you think he knew?" Paul asked his dad. "Do you think Hammy realised that the house was being burgled, and struggled to get out to bite through the burglar-alarm wires?"

His dad laughed. "No," he said. "It's a nice idea, but Hammy is only a hamster, Paul."

Paul covered Hammy's ears. Only a hamster! What a way to talk! Then, lovingly, he put Hammy back in his cage. It was only then that Paul saw them. They must have been hidden before, but now he could see them quite clearly, glinting among the bedding. Shiny, glittering gold, red and silver.

"Mum!" he cried excitedly. "Mum! Come and look!"

His mum came rushing over. And then she burst into tears. "My rings!" she cried. "Hammy has got my rings! He must have collected them. Just like he did with Jenny's play people. What a clever hamster! He even hid them so the burglars wouldn't find them!"

Paul reached inside and took the rings out. He turned to his dad.

"Still think Hammy didn't know what was going on?" he asked.

His dad shook his head. "I don't know!" he said. "I just don't know!"

Paul grinned. He did!

The next day, the whole school wanted to know every single detail about the burglary. Paul stood in front in assembly, Hammy in his hands, and told them everything that had happened. And especially about brave and clever Hammy. Everyone was impressed. Even Sam.

"Wow!" he said. "That's some hamster! Wasn't Hammy frightened at all?"

"No," said Paul. "I don't think he had time."

"Didn't you hear the burglars?" asked Anne-Marie.

"No," said Paul. "Nobody heard a thing until the burglar alarm went off."

"It seems as though we don't need guard

dogs any more," said Miss Biggs. "Just guard hamsters!"

Everyone laughed.

"Why do you think Hammy was able to take the rings and hide them, without the burglars realising what was going on?" she asked.

Julie put up her hand.

"Because he was so small!" she said. "They probably didn't even see him."

"And he had to be small to climb out of his cage in the first place!" said Paul.

"Quite!" said Miss Biggs. "So there's a lot to be said for being small, isn't there?"

Everyone looked at Paul, one of the smallest boys in the whole school, and he went red.

"Let's give Hammy three cheers!" said
Miss Biggs. And they did. But they didn't
stop at three, they gave him six!

"Hey, Titch, er, Paul!" called Sam, as they walked out of assembly.

Paul turned.

"I'm sorry I was rude about your hamster," Sam said. "He's really magic."

"That's OK," said Paul, stroking Hammy proudly.

"Oh, and I'm sorry I called you Titch all the time," said Sam.

"Oh, that's all right!" grinned Paul. He looked down at Hammy and then back up at Sam. "Actually you can call me Titch whenever you like. After all, it's good to be small!"